This book belongs to:

_____

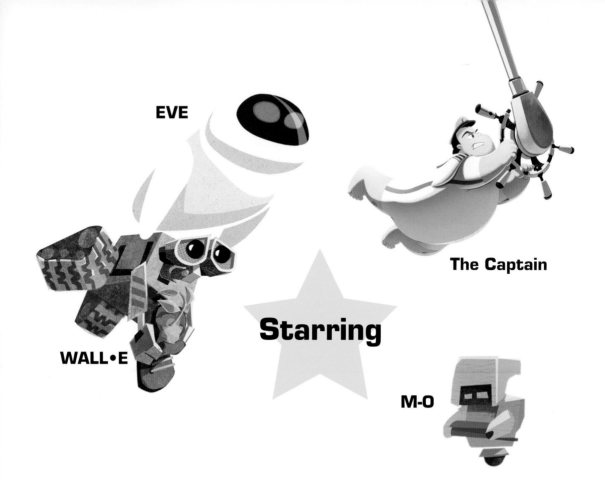

EVE

The Captain

Starring

WALL•E

M-O

First published by Parragon in 2008
Parragon
Queen Street House
4 Queen Street
Bath BA1 1HE, UK

ISBN 978-1-4075-1846-6

Printed in Italy

DISNEP · PIXAR

WALL·E

PaRragon

Bath · New York · Singapore · Hong Kong · Cologne · Delhi · Melbourne

If you had lived back in the 29th century, you would have lived off in space with all the other people from Earth. Long ago, Earth had been evacuated because it was too polluted. No one could live there until someone cleaned up the planet. And there was someone – just one – left behind to do that work.

WALL•E was a Waste Allocation Load Lifter, Earth-class. He didn't mind his lonely job of compacting trash. He looked at it as a sort of treasure hunt. He never knew what he would find each day in the trash.

But WALL•E wanted more in life. He didn't ask for much. He just wanted to hold hands with someone – someone he loved. He had seen this watching his favourite movie over and over. It was his dream.

One day, WALL•E was out compacting and cubing trash when he found something special. It was a plant. His pet cockroach chirped, knowing that his master was really interested in this green thing. Neither one of them had ever seen anything like it before. WALL•E took it home.

Soon afterwards, another robot landed on Earth. WALL•E fell in love with the sleek new robot at first sight. Her name was EVE, and over time, WALL•E figured out that she was looking for something on Earth. But she wouldn't tell him what it was.

WALL•E took her to his home and showed her all the treasures he had collected from the trash.

But when WALL•E showed her the plant, she grabbed it from him and stored it in a secret compartment in her chest. Then she shut down. She slept and slept, no matter how hard WALL•E tried to wake her up.

Soon EVE's ship returned to take her away. No! WALL•E loved her. He didn't want her to leave. So he latched onto the outside of her ship and followed her into space.

The spaceship docked inside an enormous ship called the *Axiom*. The Captain's robot assistant, Gopher, wrapped EVE in energy bands and drove her away. WALL•E raced after her. And M-O, a cleaner-bot, chased WALL•E. (M-O was programmed to clean, clean, clean. WALL•E, the little trash-compacting robot from Earth, was his biggest challenge ever.)

As WALL•E chased EVE, he accidentally disabled passenger Mary's electronic system. Mary blinked and looked around. She saw the world around her, instead of viewing it all digitally over her holo-screen. She liked the change.

Finally EVE was ready to give the plant to the Captain. By doing so, she would prove that Earth was clean enough that a plant could now grow there. That meant everyone could return to the planet.

But EVE's compartment was empty. The plant had disappeared!

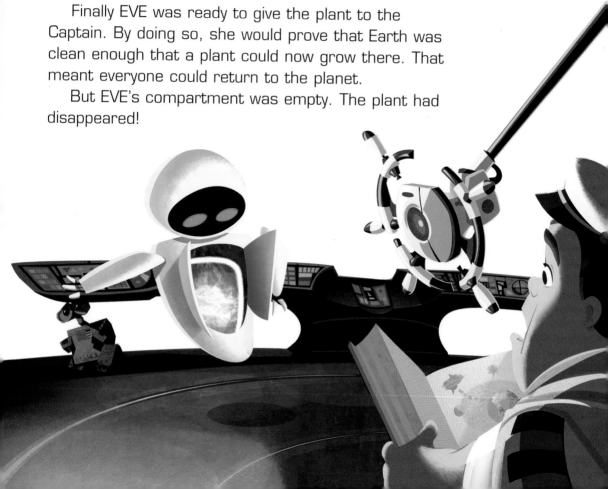

Disappointed, the Captain sent EVE to the repair ward, along with WALL•E. When they got there, WALL•E thought some orderlies were hurting EVE. So he helped her escape, along with all the reject-bots from the repair ward.

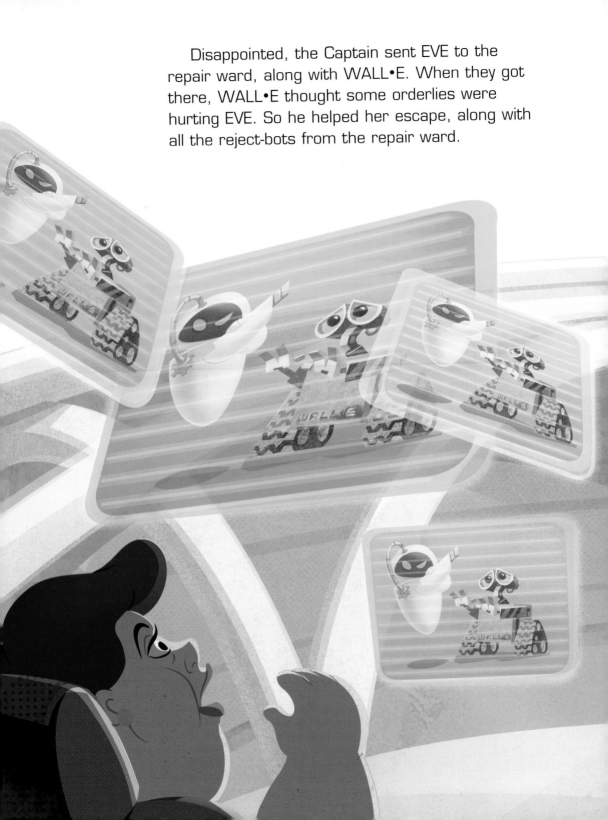

But there was a problem. Once they ran free, they looked like escaped convicts. A warning broadcast their escape throughout the *Axiom*. The ship's stewards tried to catch them.

To avoid being captured, EVE took WALL•E to an escape pod.
She would send him to Earth where he would be safe, and then she
could find the plant. Instead, Gopher appeared. He had the plant!
He put it in the escape pod. WALL•E and the plant were launched
into space – not towards Earth, but far into outer space! WALL•E
panicked and pushed a lot of buttons.

WALL•E pushed the wrong button. The pod exploded, but he escaped. EVE went to try to help him. **Whoosh!** WALL•E zoomed up to EVE . . . and showed her that he had saved the plant. Delighted, she leaned in towards him, and an arc of electricity passed between their foreheads – a robot kiss.

Soon they were floating
in space, dancing and giggling.

Back on the *Axiom*, WALL•E tried to wait as EVE delivered the plant to the Captain. The Captain was so excited that he was ready to return to Earth, but Auto wouldn't let him.

Quickly Gopher snatched the plant and dumped it down the trash chute. It hit WALL•E. The little bot was climbing up to get to EVE. Happily he delivered the plant right to her. But Auto electrocuted WALL•E and sent him back down the chute with EVE.

WALL•E and EVE ended up in the ship's garbage bay. EVE rescued the injured little bot while WALL•E tried to give her the plant. He still thought she wanted it more than anything else. But WALL•E was wrong. EVE just wanted to help WALL•E now. M-O helped, still trying to clean WALL•E.

Soon EVE flew all three of them
up and out of the garbage bay, with the
plant in hand. Now she wanted the plant
to get WALL•E home to Earth – to his
truck home – to find the right parts and
fix him.

The Captain was fighting Auto for
control of the ship by now. He sent a message
to EVE, telling her to take the plant to a large machine
called the holo-detector. It would scan the plant and
ready the ship to head towards Earth. That was all EVE
cared about now.

The Captain was amazing. He stood up on his own for the first time in his life. He fought against Auto. He activated the holo-detector. And he finally managed to turn off Auto's power.

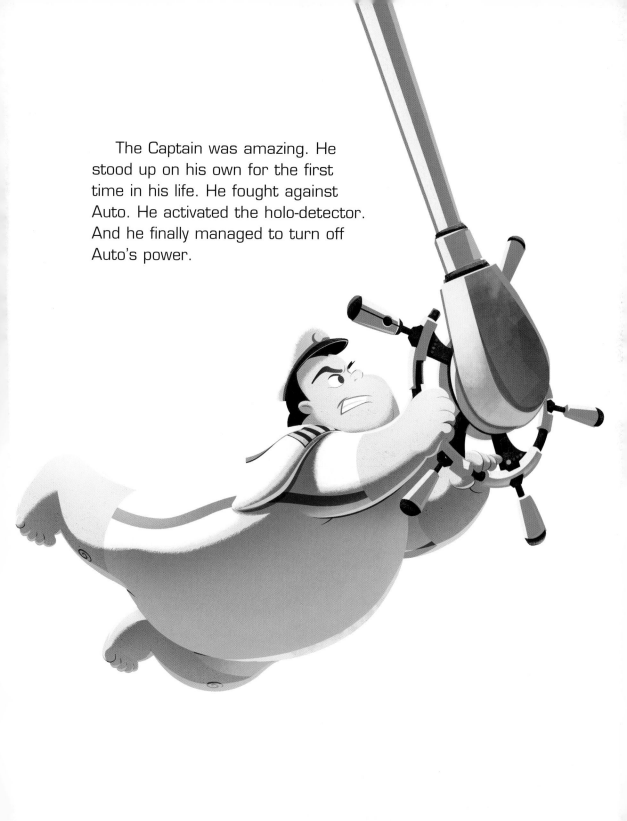

EVE fought to reach the holo-detector. At last she put the plant inside the machine. The holo-detector scanned the plant. Finally they could return to Earth.

But not all was well. WALL•E had been crushed by the giant machine, trying to keep it up high enough.

Heartbroken, EVE pulled WALL•E's crushed body from under the holo-detector.

More determined than before, EVE wanted to take him home to his truck where she could find the right parts to bring him back to life.

As soon as the *Axiom* landed on Earth, EVE headed straight for WALL•E's home and began to repair him. At last, he powered up . . . and began cubing trash. Something was wrong. He was just another trash-cubing robot. All the love was gone. He didn't even recognize EVE.

Sadly, EVE held WALL•E's hand and leaned towards him.

An electric arc passed between their heads – the robot kiss. She was saying good-bye.

Then . . . WALL•E's hand began to move. EVE looked into his eyes. He was coming back to life! He recognized her!

"Ee-vah?" he said.

After following EVE across the universe, WALL•E had ended up right where he had started: home. But this time, he had the one thing he had always wanted – EVE's hand clasped in his own.